WEEKLY READER BOOKS presents

What Is a Jungle?

A **Just Ask**™ Book

Hi, my name is
Christopher!

by Chris Arvetis
and Carole Palmer

illustrated by
James Buckley

FIELD PUBLICATIONS
MIDDLETOWN, CT.

I can hardly walk.
The plants are very
thick here.
Where in the world am I?

I know where I am!

You're in a
JUNGLE !
The word "jungle"
means a place with
many tropical plants.

The green on the map
shows the jungles
all over the world.

Jungles get lots
of sunshine.

It is very hot and
it stays warm all
year long.

EUROPE

NORTH
AMERICA

AFRICA

Equator

SOUTH
AMERICA

Jungles also get lots of rain.
It seems like there is a shower almost every day.

It sure is hot and wet. And there are so many plants.

Remember, the word jungle means a place with lots of plants.

It is really another name for a tropical RAIN FOREST.

A rain forest has many plants and trees.

The tall trees have thick layers of leaves at the top. The jungle always stays green because the trees grow new leaves as soon as old ones fall off.

Many of the trees have flowers that grow right out of the branches and trunks.

Look at the beautiful ones here.

Plants that grow at
the top of a tree are
called air plants.

They need to be high up
so that they can get
more sunlight.

Besides the hundreds of beautiful plants, there are many animals.
Maybe you'll know some of them.
I know most of them!

High above us a sloth looks down at the armadillo on the rock.

Over there, a spider monkey swings on the branch.

Look at the tiny tree frog sunning itself on this leaf. The iguana also likes to sun itself.

Some of the most beautiful creatures here are the birds.

See the two toucans with the large beaks and the colorful macaw.

The tiny hummingbirds and butterflies are colorful, too.

Beautiful !

I keep away from the boa constrictor curled around the branch.
And the tarantula on the leaf.
And the jaguar in the grass.

An anteater is down there, too.

These pictures are animals
that live in other jungles.
Here is a tiger.

This big one is an orangutan and the other one is a chimpanzee.

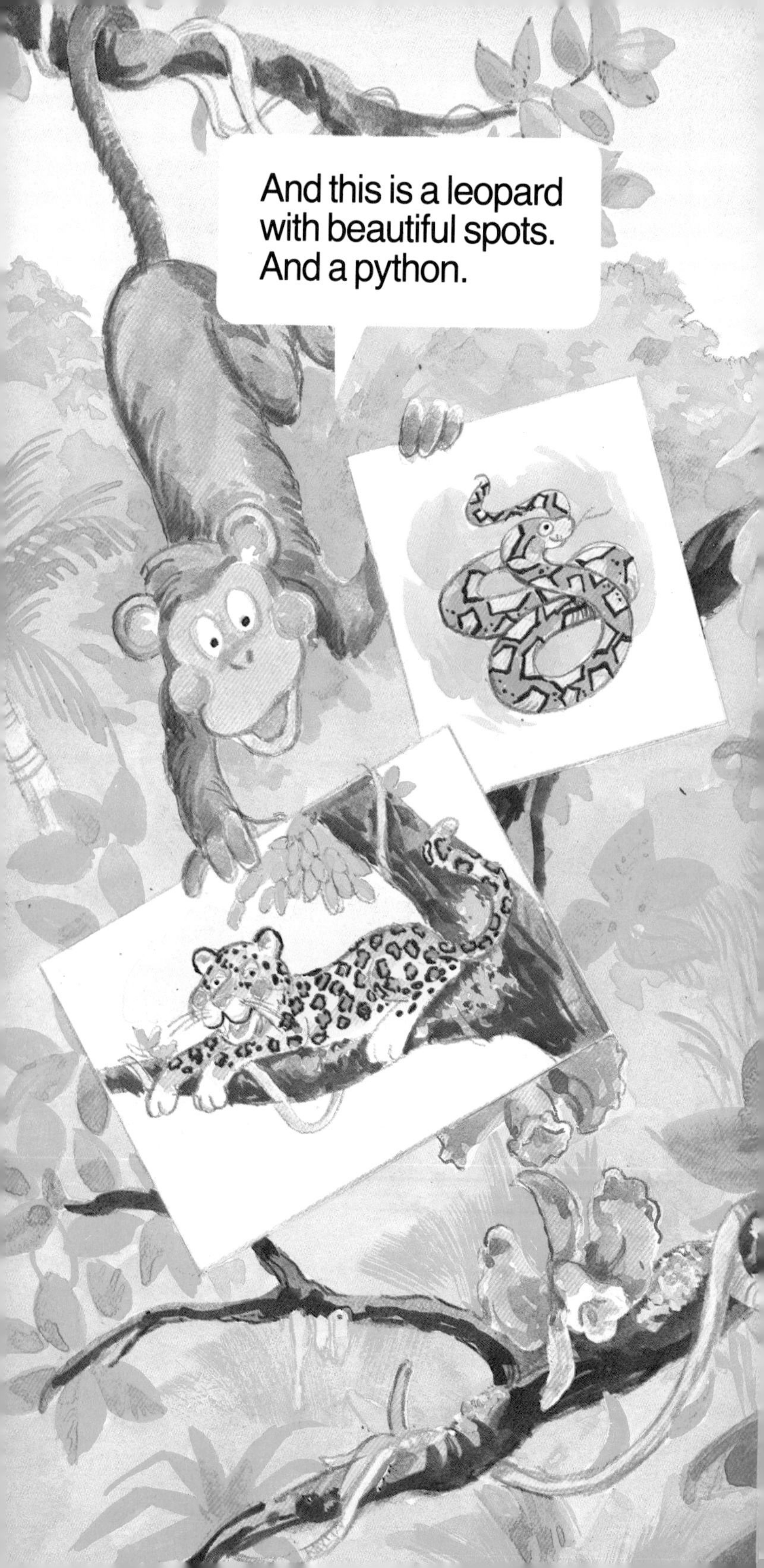
And this is a leopard with beautiful spots. And a python.

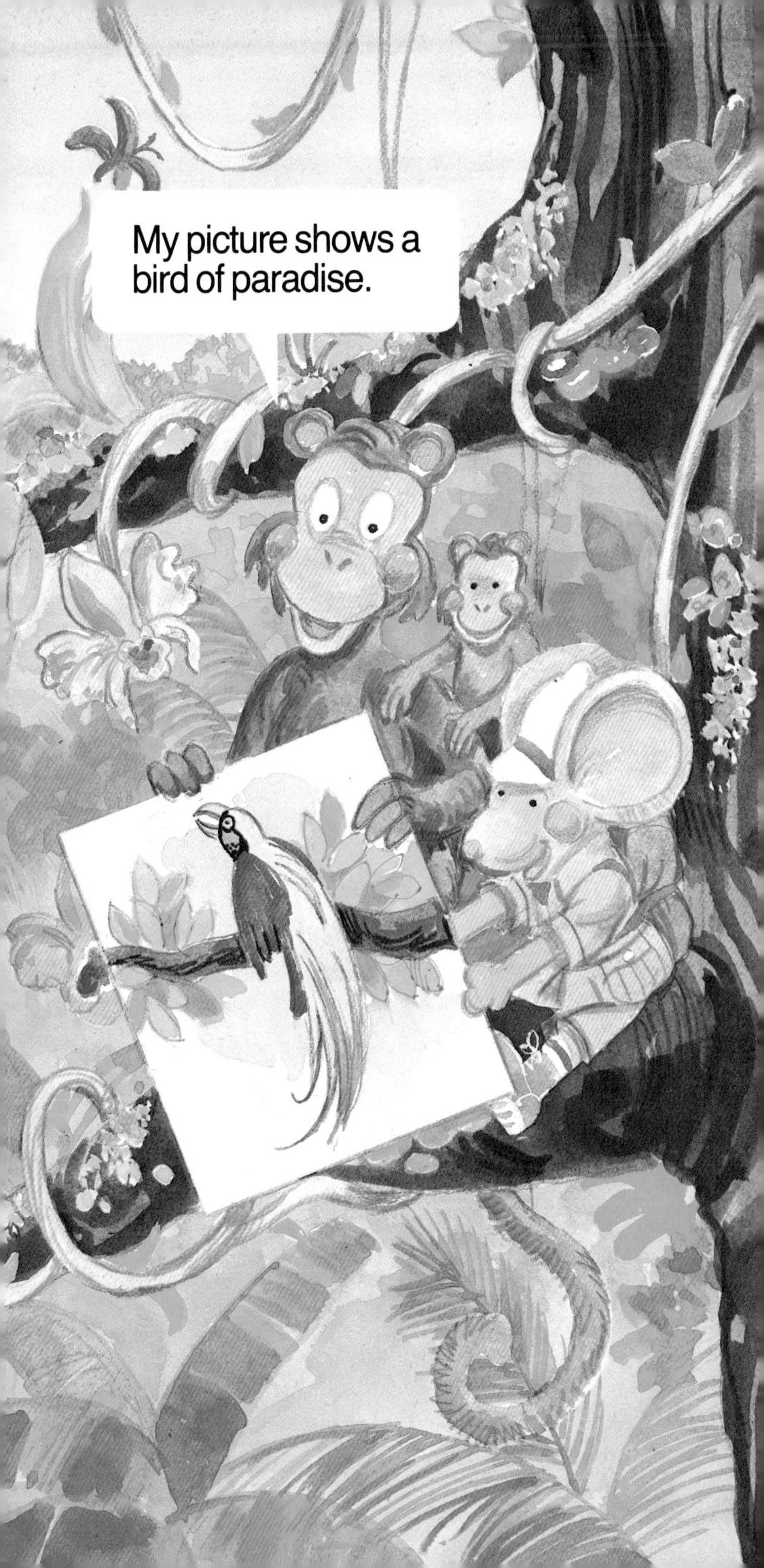
My picture shows a bird of paradise.

So a jungle is a name for a plant-filled, tree-filled rain forest.

The warm climate and the wet weather make excellent living conditions for all these plants and animals.

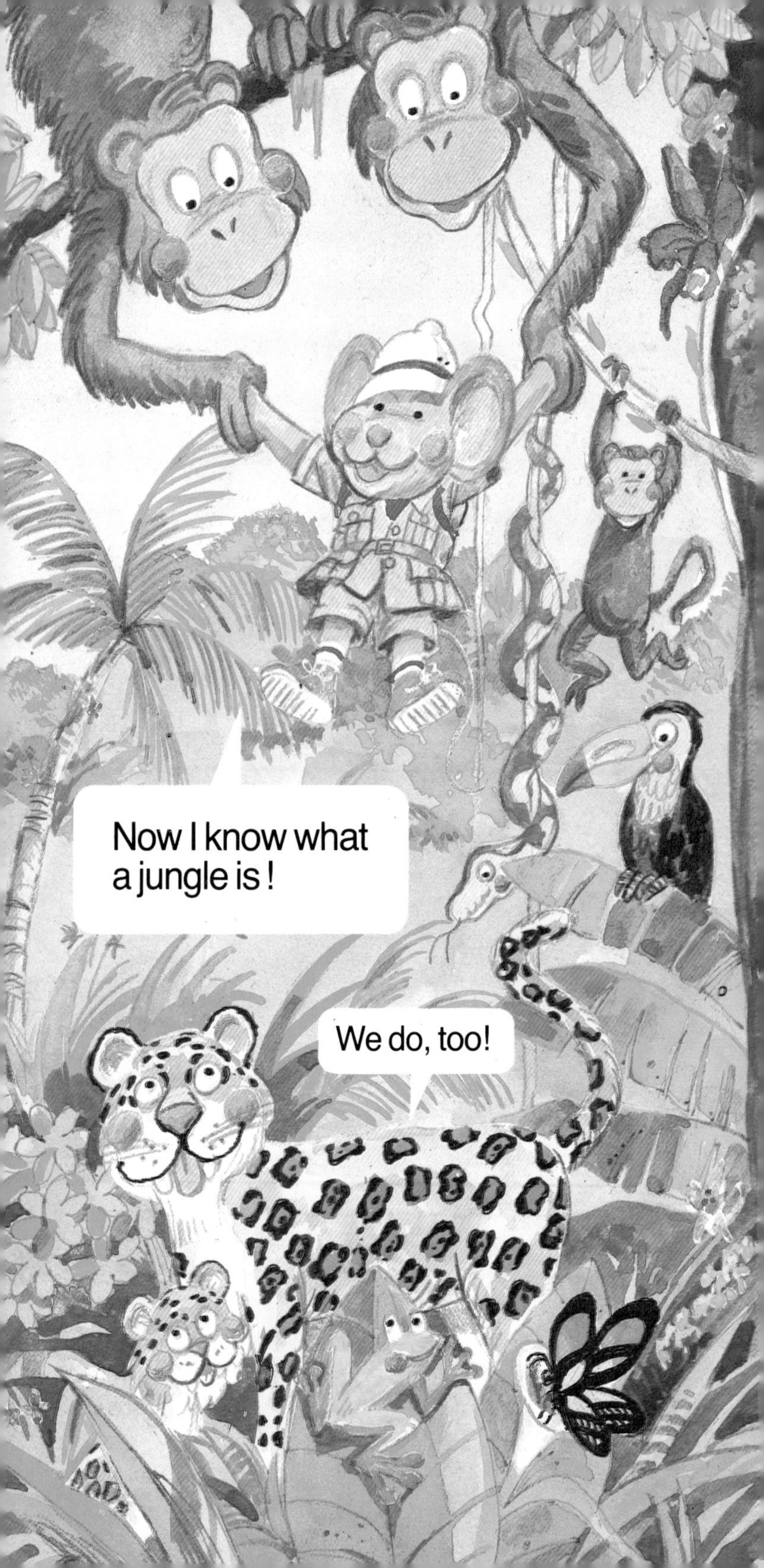
Now I know what a jungle is!
We do, too!